Two Mice in a Boat

Published by Pleasant Company Publications
First published in Great Britain by Penguin Books Ltd., 2002
© 2003 Helen Craig Limited and Katharine Holabird
Based on the text by Katharine Holabird and the illustrations by Helen Craig
From the script by Barbara Slade

Visit our Web site at www.americangirl.com and
Angelina's very own site at www.angelinaballerina.com

Printed in the U.S.A.

02 03 04 05 06 07 08 NGS 10 9 8 7 6 5 4 3 2 1

Angelina™
Ballerina

Two Mice in a Boat

PLEASANT
COMPANY
PUBLICATIONS™

It was bedtime, but Angelina wasn't tired. She'd found her father's old Miller's Pond Boat Carnival trophy.

"Oh, Dad! I'm determined to win this year," she said.

"And how are you going to decorate your boat, Angelina?" asked her father.

"Well," began Angelina, "it will be a huge white swan, with gold thrones for Alice and me, the Swan Princesses!"

"It sounds lovely, dear, but don't count on being teamed up with Alice," warned Mrs. Mouseling gently.

The next day at school, Miss Chalk announced the boat-decorating teams. "Priscilla with Penelope, Flora with William, Angelina with Sammy . . ."

"Sammy!" said Angelina, shocked.

"Angelina!" sputtered Sammy.

"Alice with Henry," continued Miss Chalk. Alice looked horrified.

"It's all about teamwork!" said Miss Chalk over the din of unhappy mice.

Angelina and Sammy lined up to collect their boat from Captain Miller.

"I wouldn't be seen dead in a sissy swan boat," muttered Sammy.

"Well, you wouldn't catch me on some stupid pirate ship!" spat Angelina. She sighed as she looked at Sammy's plans. "We're never going to agree, so we'll just have to try and . . ."

"Work together," they both muttered.

The next day, they drew a line down the middle of the boat. They decided to decorate one-half each. "Don't go over the line," warned Angelina sternly.

"Don't worry, I won't!" said Sammy.

Down near the river, Alice and Henry were decorating their boat with sweets.

"One for the boat, one for you!" they said happily, popping candies into each other's mouths.

On the day of the carnival, Angelina and Sammy got ready
early and went to try out their boat on the river.

"It floats!" cried Angelina when they eventually managed
to launch it.

The two mice turned around when they heard a rumbling noise behind them. It was the builder mouse, Mr. Ratchett.

"Nice boat you've got there!" he said. "What's she called?"

"The Swan Princess," said Angelina.

"The Pirate King!" shouted Sammy.

"That's a big name for a small boat!" chuckled Mr. Ratchett as he carried on up the road.

The mouselings jumped on board.

"I think we're sinking," said Sammy as he watched water seeping into the boat.

"I said that cannon was too heavy!" cried Swan Princess Angelina furiously.

"It's probably that stupid bird's head," muttered Pirate Sammy.

They began to throw things out of the boat as fast as they could, until there was absolutely nothing left.

"We're floating now!" said Sammy.

"Downstream!" shouted Angelina desperately. "Where are the oars?"

"Over there!" cried Sammy, pointing to the oars floating away in the water.

Meanwhile, Alice and Henry had nearly finished their boat, but they'd spent quite a lot of time eating the decorations and felt a little sick!

Farther downstream, Angelina and Sammy were moving fast!

"We've got to stop!" yelled Angelina.

"I can see a tree stump up ahead!" bellowed Sammy.

"We need some rope to loop over it. Look!" Angelina had seen something.

"Vines!" they both said together.

As the little boat sped along, the two frightened mice grabbed onto the vines.

"Hold on!" shouted Sammy.

The vines broke away from the bank, and Angelina found the longest one. Angelina and Sammy both grabbed onto it just as the boat reached the tree stump.

They struggled to loop the vine over the stump and pulled themselves onto the bank.

"We have to get back to Miller's Pond!" cried a desperate Angelina.

Just then, Sammy and Angelina heard a *chug chug* behind them.

"Mr. Ratchett!" they both shouted, relieved.

At Miller's Pond, the carnival was under way. Alice and Henry were dressed as candy canes, and their boat was decorated entirely with candy wrappers!

Suddenly there was a distant chugging noise, and everybody turned to look.

It was Swan Princess Angelina and Pirate Sammy. They were floating along in the sky on the end of Mr. Ratchett's crane!

Everyone at Miller's Pond clapped and cheered as Angelina and Sammy were slowly lowered toward the water.

SPLASH! They landed a bit too close to Priscilla and
Penelope Pinkpaws' boat. It was decorated as a huge pink
ballet shoe. "Our lovely shoe!" they squeaked. "Now it's
soaking wet!"

Angelina and Sammy giggled together.

"The winners of the boat-decorating contest are Alice and
Henry," said Captain Miller a little later. "But this year's
prize for teamwork goes to Angelina and Sammy!"

Mr. Mouseling introduced Angelina to his old boating
partner — Sammy's dad! "We never won a teamwork
prize," said Mr. Watts. "We were always arguing."

"No we weren't!" replied Mr. Mouseling.

Angelina and Sammy giggled.

"YOU keep the trophy," said Angelina.

"No, you keep it," replied Sammy.

The two mouselings, and their fathers, carried on arguing and laughing until the sun went down and it was time for every tired mouse to go home to bed.